# YAK AND GNU

## Juliette MacIver

## ILLUSTRATED BY
## Cat Chapman

CANDLEWICK PRESS

This is Yak, this is Gnu—
the best of friends,
dear and true.

Yak has a kayak,
Gnu a canoe.
Yak's is black.
Gnu's is blue.

Yak and Gnu
love to row
down the river.
Off they go!

Yak in a kayak, blackberry black,
Gnu in a blueberry-blue canoe,
sing a sea song that's sung by two:

"Yippee-ai, Yak!"
"Woo-hoo, Gnu!"
"There's nobody else
like me and you.
No one else
but you and me
can float a boat
or sail the sea."

"Yoo-hoo, Yak!
G'day, Gnu!"

"A goat in a boat?
That can't be true!"

"He's sailing, yes,"
Gnu began,
"but still, that's only
THREE who can."

"Yippee-ai, Yak!"
"Woo-hoo, Gnu!"
"There's nobody else
like me and you.
(Well, only Goat.)"

"What the hoo?
Look, Gnu!

"A snazzy snail
setting sail . . .

"and a laughing calf
aboard a raft."

"A snail? A calf?
Jumpin' jive!
Along with Goat,
that makes five.
Only FIVE
can sail thus:
Snail and Calf
and Goat and us!"

"Yippee-ai, Yak!"
"Woo-hoo, Gnu!"
"There's nobody else
like me and you.
(Well, only Goat,
Snail, and Calf.)"

"By gack, there's more!"
said Yak. "I saw
a nasty stingy
on a rusty dinghy . . .

"a stout pig afloat
on an outrigger boat,
and a rat and her clan
on a catamaran!"

"Oh, well," said Gnu.
"At any rate,
with Scorpion, Pig,
and Rat to date,
sailing boats
just total EIGHT."

"Yippee-ai, Yak!"
"Woo-hoo, Gnu!"
"There's nobody else
like me and you!
(Well, only Goat, Snail, Calf,
Scorpion, Pig, and Rat.)"

"LOOK OUT!" cried Yak.
"Starboard tack.
That hippopotamus
would have gotten us!"

Good grief!
What's next?
They're most perplexed.
How can it be?
But here they see
a gorilla sail with
a humpback whale.
Not one gorilla . . .

but a whole FLOTILLA!

And a herd of giraffes
on hovercrafts!

And an ocean cruise
full of yaks and gnus!

"Our song is wrong!"
Yak stamped and wept.
"There's nobody else
like us EXCEPT

goats and snails, gorillas, whales,

pigs, giraffes, hippos, calfs,

scorpions, rats, and hold your hats—

stacks and stacks
of gnus and yaks!"

"But does it matter?"
smiled Gnu.
"Who cares, my friend,
when I have you."

So Yak took his kayak
(blackberry black),
Gnu her canoe
(blueberry blue),
and they sang a sea song
that's sung by two:

For my dear brother and sister in law, Nick and
Alex; and my darling nieces, Isabella, Pippa, and
Lottie. There's nobody else quite like you!

J. M.

For Thurston and his little brother, Miles

C. C.

First U.S. edition 2015

Library of Congress Catalog Card Number 2013957525
ISBN 978-0-7636-7561-5

15 16 17 18 19 20 CCP 10 9 8 7 6 5 4 3 2 1

Printed in Shenzhen, Guangdong, China

This book was typeset in Coming Soon.
The illustrations were done in ink and watercolor.

Candlewick Press
99 Dover Street
Somerville, Massachusetts 02144

visit us at www.candlewick.com